Next Please

Ernst Jandl and Norman Junge

First published in the United Kingdom in 2001

1 3 5 7 9 10 8 6 4 2

Text © Hermann Luchterhand Verlag GmbH & Co KG, Darmstadt and Neuwied 1970
First published in Germany by Luchterhand Literaturverlag, Munich in 1970
fünfter sein © Beltz Verlag, Weinham and Basel 1997
Programm Beltz & Gelberg, Weinheim
Translation © Hutchinson Children's Books 2001

First published in the United Kingdom in 2001 by
Hutchinson Children's Books
The Random House Group Limited
20 Vauxhall Bridge Road, London SW1V 2SA

Random House Australia (Pty) Limited
20 Alfred Street, Milsons Point, Sydney
New South Wales 2061, Australia

Random House New Zealand Limited
18 Poland Road, Glenfield
Auckland 10, New Zealand

Random House South Africa (Pty) Limited
Endulini, 5A Jubilee Road, Parktown 2193, South Africa

The Random House Group Limited Reg. No. 954009

www.randomhouse.co.uk

A CIP catalogue record for this book
is available from the British Library

ISBN: 0 09 176958 2

Printed in Hong Kong

Next Please

Ernst Jandl and Norman Junge

HUTCHINSON

London Sydney Auckland Johannesburg

Five are waiting.

Door opens.
One comes out.

"Next, please."
One goes in.

Four waiting.

Door opens.
One comes out.

"Next, please."
One goes in.

Three waiting.

Door opens.
One comes out.

"Next, please."
One goes in.

Two waiting.

Door opens.
One comes out.

"Next, please."
One goes in.

One waiting.
All alone.

Door opens.
One comes out.

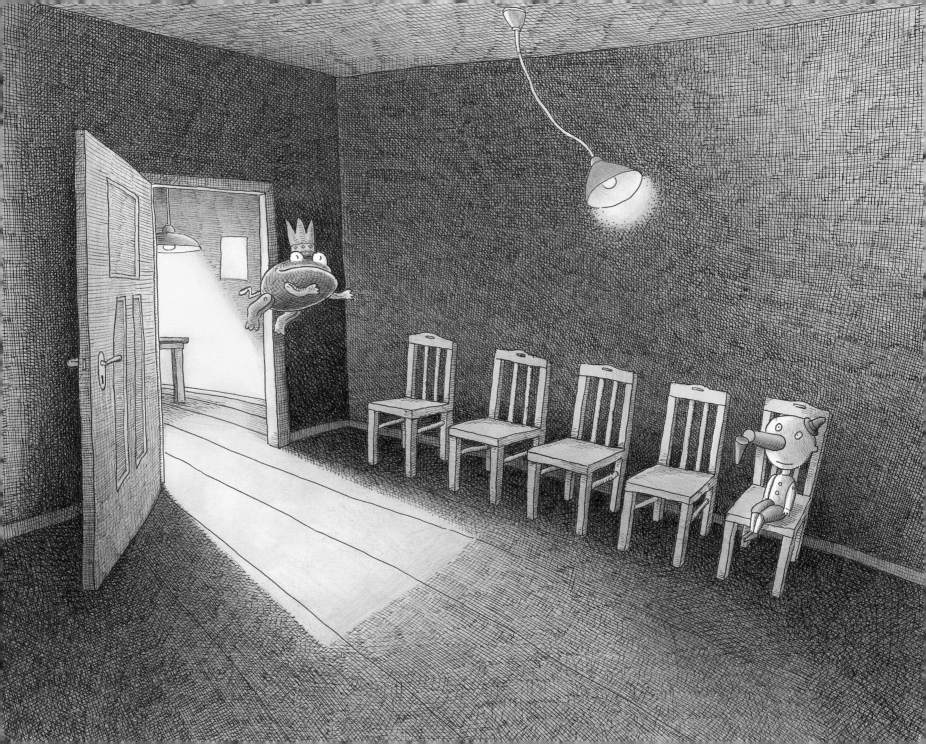

"Next, please."
Last one goes in.

"Hello, young fellow, are you the last one?"
"Yes, Doctor. None waiting."